THE PURPLE PORPOISE PRESERVES THE PLANET WITH A 'P'

By
Jim
Peluso

Dear Sarah,
Here's hoping all your dreams come true,
Best Wishes,
Jim Peluso

12/24/07

Publisher's Cataloging-in-Publication
(Provided by Quality Books, Inc.)

Peluso, Jim.
  The purple porpoise preserves the planet with a "P" /
written and illustrated by Jim Peluso.
  p. cm.
  SUMMARY: After falling asleep in a field, a young man
meets a porpoise that can make anything appear or
disappear with the help of a magic wand and a command
beginning with the letter P. The porpoise and the man
use the wand to defeat an evil king.
  LCCN 2007902640
  ISBN-13: 978-0-9795172-1-1
  ISBN-10: 0-9795172-1-4

  1. Porpoises--Juvenile fiction. 2. Magic--Juvenile
fiction. 3. P (The letter)--Juvenile fiction.
[1. Porpoises--Fiction. 2. Magic--Fiction. 3. P (The
letter)--Fiction. 4. Alphabet--Fiction. 5. Stories in
rhyme.] I. Title.

PZ8.3.P45Pur 2007   [Fic]
                    QBI07-600162

THE PURPLE PORPOISE PRESERVES THE PLANET WITH A 'P'

written and illustrated by
Jim Peluso

Published by:
✒Angelcrest Publishing
P.O. Box 27
Syosset, NY 11791-4924

Library of Congress Control Number: 2007902640
ISBN-13: 978-0-9795172-1-1

One summer's noon
near the end of June
as I laid in a field
of tall grass,
the midsummer's heat
put me to sleep
and into a dream-world
I passed. . .

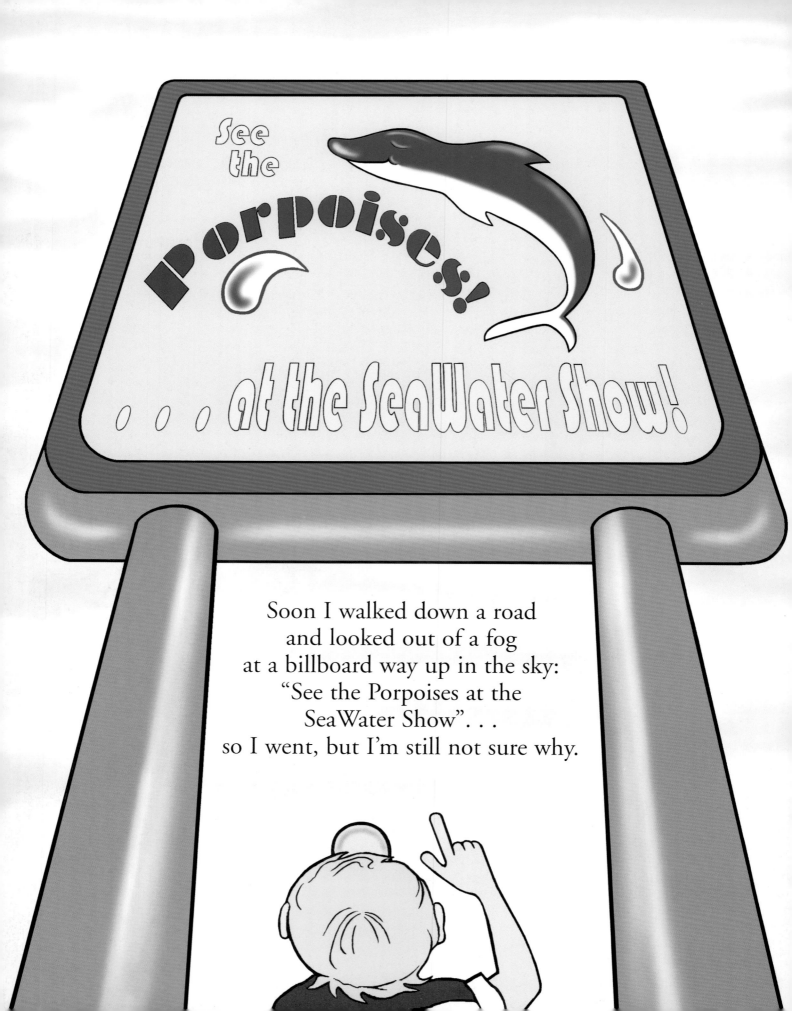

Soon I walked down a road
and looked out of a fog
at a billboard way up in the sky:
"See the Porpoises at the
SeaWater Show". . .
so I went, but I'm still not sure why.

When I arrived at the show I saw porpoises there
of all sizes and shapes, jumping hoops in the air.
They were all colored blue with the fittest of fin,
yet I watched this old fish who just
sat there and grinned.

He looked so proud and prim
in his tophat and tie
and his monocle sat
quite firm in one eye.
As he reached in his case
for an item or two,
I noticed this porpoise
was purple!
. . . not blue!

Well I rubbed my poor eyes as I knew I was dreaming,
when all of a sudden the crowd started screaming!
This porpoise walked right to the spotlight and
bowed, then cleared out his throat and spoke
right out loud!

"Dear pupils of mine," he said to the crowd
in an elegant tone and a wipe of his brow.
"Please be so kind as to let me reveal
a magical secret we porpoises conceal!"

Then he held
to the crowd a
purplish "P",
which perhaps held
some magic, or at least
so thought he. . .

"A porpoise you see,
as brilliant as me
can do wonderful things
with a wand shaped
like "P".

The crowd fell to a hush as this porpoise droned on,
but I wasn't impressed with his prose or his con. . .
in fact I found him a little too smug, so I
jumped from my seat to confront the big lug!
But something he said gave my heart
a small tug. . .

"Rule One of the Purple Porpoise's creed,"
cried the porpoise who was very
purple indeed. . .
"purpose, precision and personality
make porpoises the world's most
intelligent breed.
You'll notice the key's in the
fair letter "P",
the most pleasing letter
there ever could be!"

I knew as he spoke on,
this sea-creature of charm
was someone I had to
know better.
So I crept closer to peek,
yet hoping to speak
to this porpoise
about this
"P" letter.

"Excuse me sir ", I said to the porpoise
as he finished his speech to the crowd.
"Could you tell me more about this "P" wand?"
And he said, "my prawn I'd be proud!"

Just then the sky above turned to gray
and the big crowd started to leave.
But I stayed right there with the porpoise,
. . . in fact I was starting to cleave!

"Tsk, tsk, little prawn!" he started to scold
as the clouds above started to sprinkle. . .
"don't you know to get out of the rain? . .
your shirt has become quite a wrinkle!"

And with a flick of the wrist
with that "P" in his fist,
my shirt was all pressed in a twinkle!

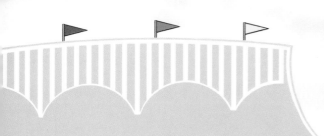

"My goodness" I shouted in wonder and awe
as my shirt looked much better than new.
"How did you do that and how does it work
with that letter of purplish hue?"

"You see", he began, "this key that I hold,
shaped in the fair letter "P"
is the power of old of which I have told,
–outlined in the porpoise's creed."

Well I didn't quite follow
but did understand
that the wand that he
waved over me
could bring about all
you could ever command,
–provided it started
with "P".

"*Pressed*" I declared as I nearly fell down.
"You said "pressed" as the wand passed my shirt!
And "pressed" is a word that begins with a "P"
—and it also *pushed* out the dirt!"

"Precisely my prawn. . .you're really perceiving!"
the proud purple porpoise rejoiced.
"Now come with me and I'll have you believing!"
So I went, not feeling much choice. . .

"Perhaps you'd like a palace of paisley" he posed,
". . . painted in purple and pink."
And I picked the place to be Paris. . .
—he could see I was starting to think!

We were there in a flash with our passports in hand
when he caught me off guard in a strange foreign land:
"Hungry for something?" he posed with a smile,
but he knew my response would be hasty,
so before I could say the words "ice cream"
he stopped me and shouted out "pastry!"

Pies of peaches, plums and pears
and patties of pistachios and peanuts were there!

"This is delicious!" I said as I gobbled,
and that purple fish ate so much
he just wobbled!

When we were full I was ready for fun
and suggested we go in the palace.
But the porpoise warned of a king who lived there
who was wicked and full of malice!

"You see little prawn," the porp warmly warned,
"the things this "P" letter invents,
don't always turn out to be good,
. . . though made with the best of intents."

Well he pulled me along to the palace's door
and I knocked hoping no one would answer,
when we were approached by a knight on a horse,
. . . apparently he was a lancer. . .

"Whom do you seek?" growled the knight with a snarl
as I tried not to show I was shaking.
"We'd like a tour!" said the porp with a roar
and the knight said "it's yours for the taking!"

As we entered inside
this palace so wide,
made by the Porpoise's "P",
I paused as a person performed
and a piper piped tunes playfully.

There were pandas and
panthers and parrots,
and portraits that
hung on the wall,
and as I peeked in the distance,
I saw a parade down the hall!

"You see", said the knight, "the king has been mad,
mad as mad can be,
since the day he lost his powerful wand
—shaped in the fair letter "P"!"

Well I shrieked as I looked at the porpoise,
and noticed his eyes got quite swollen. . .
the knight said the *king* made these things with that "P"
and now the great wand has been stolen! . .

Well my heart sunk inside and tears came to my eyes
as the poor porpoise offered relief:
"Don't worry little prawn", he whispered,
"I assure you, I'm not the thief!"

When the knight went to clean a horse for the queen
the porpoise began to explain:

"Little prawn understand that this king has a plan,
and one that is evil, you'll see. . .
he wants to take over the *planet!*
. . . and he once stole this letter from me!"

"Then he started to make himself all that you see
as he found the "P" wand brought him power and glee,
but his heart was not good and he wouldn't stop there
'til he conquered the earth and robbed all of us bare!"

"So I brought you along", the porpoise confessed,
"to help me to try and straighten this mess! . .
if the king got a hold of this letter my friend,
the great planet earth could come to an end!"

"And as for this palace", the porpoise explained,
"I must admit. . . I'm the one to blame.
I created it all with this fair letter "P"
. . . including the king with his peril,
you see?"

The porpoise spoke on, but I was alarmed
as I thought of this perilous king;
what if he found out that *we* had this "P" letter?
What evil to us would it bring?!!

"My prawn", said the porpoise, "maybe it's guilt
. . . or an inner concern for mankind,
but we must erase both this king and this place
to give you and I both peace of mind."

In puzzled despair I spoke up to the porp
as the answer to me was so clear:
"Take the wand! Say a word! We can both rest assured
that this palace will all disappear!"

"Well" said the porp as he started to blush,
trying to hide the real reason,
"maybe *you'd* like to give it a try. . .
I'm afraid this isn't my season. . ."

Well my blood boiled inside as I started to think:
this erudite porp with such manner,
was stuck for a word to erase this big place,
—and relying on *me* for the grammar!

"So that's why I'm here!" I shouted at him,
"you couldn't think of a word!
Don't tell me again how bright porpoises are,
I think there's more brains in a bird!"

Well I hollered so loud that I caused a commotion
and everyone gathered around,
. . . including the king who was full of emotion
as he looked at the porpoise and frowned. . .

"Take him!" barked the king whose eyes were afire
as he knew that the porp had the "P".
"And this little one too, —we'll make of them stew
and I'll take that "P" letter for me!"

Well the next thing I knew I was chained to a wall,
–wanting nothing to do
with that porpoise at all.

But I howled at the
porpoise who also
was chained,
"you're guilty of this,
as for me,
–I've been
framed!"

That porpoise
just hung
with his
head held
in shame!

Then in walked the king
with a sinister smile,
snickering "glad you could come,
. . .do stay awhile!"

Then he began to stir a black pot,
laughing "hope you like stew. . .
I like it a lot!"

It was no secret
we were to be dinner,
and I looked quite plump
yet that porpoise looked thinner.
He looked much too thin for his
chain I could see,
he could slip right away in a flash
and be free!

But I saw in his eyes
the porp had a surprise
for the king
as he started to tell him
some lies. . .

"Pardon me
dear king
but might
I impose?
You wouldn't
want to get ill
I suppose?"

"We porps must
be cooked in
cold water
not hot.
Or a king could
get sick
and his stomach
could rot!"

Well the king rubbed his beard and looked up once or twice,
but then thanked the porp for his friendly advice.
"But it will take *hours* for this pot to start cooling"
said the king whose mouth was already drooling.

"Not so," said the porp who was sharp as could be,
"not when you've got a magical "P"!"
So the king waved the wand over the pot
and shouted out "POOL" which cooled it alot!

"There!" said the king who stood proud on a stool,
"this water's as nice as a swimming pool!"

Just then the porpoise slipped from his chain
and dove into the water,
which splashed out like rain. . .

. . .the shock of it all took the king by surprise
as the wand flew up in the air by my eyes.
I knew that I had not a moment to cherish,
so I grabbed the "P" wand and shouted out "PERISH!"

The king knew he had made an imperial goof,
as he and the palace and people went. . .

POOF!

Well that's all I recall as I awoke in the field
and thought about porpoises and all they've concealed.

What if such a "P" letter did really exist?
The things I could do I never could list.

So maybe there's more than the porpoise's creed
boasting purpose, precision and personality. . .
perhaps with a promise of patience and prayer
we'll see a planet more precious and more people who care!

Easy Order Form

To order additional copies of this book:

☎ **Order by Phone: 1-(800) 431-1579 (BCH Fulfillment & Distribution)**

💻 **Order Online: www.angelcrst.com or www.bookch.com**

📪 **Order by Mail: Please fill out form below and mail to:**

Angelcrest Publishing
P.O. Box 27
Syosset, NY 11791-4924

✂ -

(Ship to):

Name _____

Address _____

City_____ **State** _____ **Zip** _____

Telephone (_____ **)**_____

e-mail_____

No. of books_____ **@ $14.95/ ea. = $** _____ **(Line 1)**

Shipping & Handling:
(Add $6.50 for first book & $2.50 for each   **= $** _____ **(Line 2)**
  additional book)

* Sales Tax (NY state residents only) = $ _____ **(Line 3)**
(Please add your County or City sales tax rate
  to the total of Line 1)

           Total = $ _____ **(Line 4)**

Payment Method:

Check ☐   **Money Order** ☐   **(Make payable to Angelcrest Publishing)**

Credit Card: Visa ☐   **Mastercard** ☐   **AMEX** ☐   **Other**_____

Card Number_____ **Security code**_____

Name on Card_____ **Exp. Date**_____

While most orders will be received sooner, please allow up to 3 weeks for delivery.